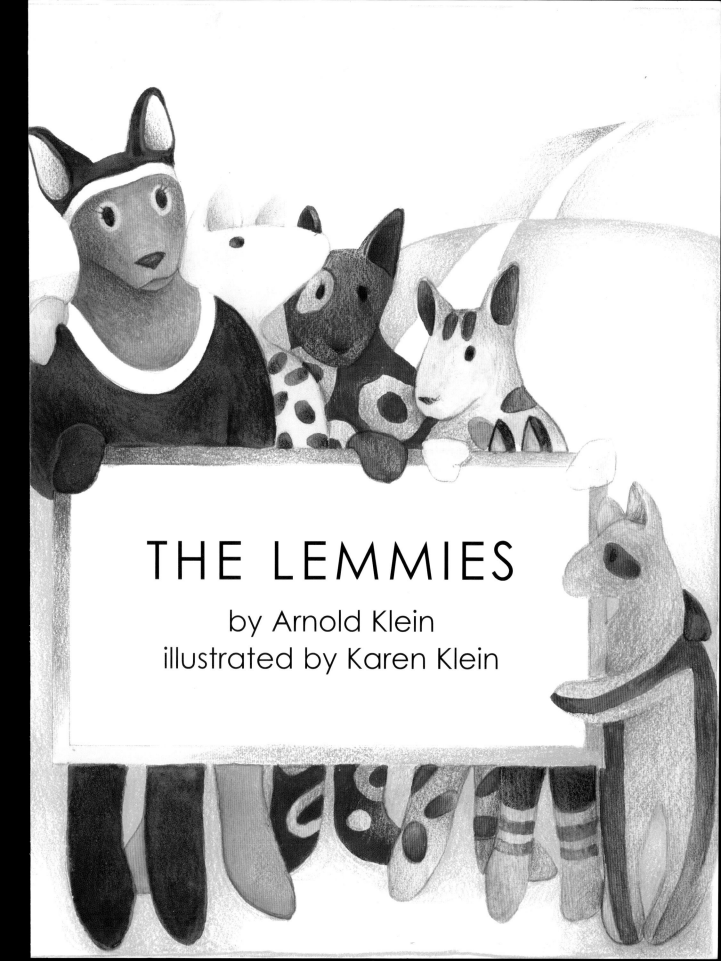

THE LEMMIES

by Arnold Klein
illustrated by Karen Klein

Library of Congress Control Number:
2004117768
The Lemmies/Arnold Klein
ISBN # 1-928623-31-X

Summary: Six little lemmies encounter a peculiar creature. Their speculation on its identity leads to unexpected results and a lesson in the appreciation of others' differences.

First Page Publications
12103 Merriman • Livonia • MI • 48150
1-800-343-3034 • Fax 734-525-4420
www.firstpagepublications.com

To our wonderful children,
Korinthia, Arno and Barrett

Six   little lemmies

ambled down
the road

to seek a singular
species of toad.

The smallest lemmie all
but shrieked

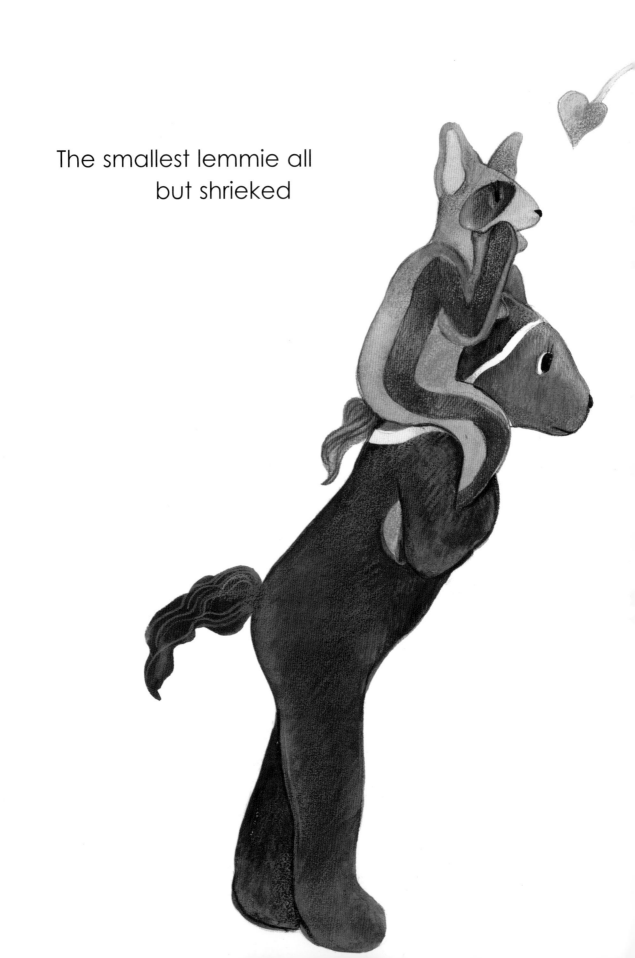

when out of a modest
      rockpile peeked

the most peculiar
      looking creature

without a sign of a
      regular feature.

"What in heaven's name is this?"
they cried,

when at last what they thought
they sought was spied.

When the undisguised
beast more fully emerged–

"Come close,
              all of you,"
it surprisingly urged.

The second smallest lemmie
            suffered dread

before this creaking,
            awkward quadruped;

he couldn't make out its
            head or tail–

it looked less like a toad
            than a primitive snail.

The third smallest lemmie was
                determined to see

if the toad had some feathers
                below the right knee;

If so it could win an
amphibian prize

as something they
could idolize.

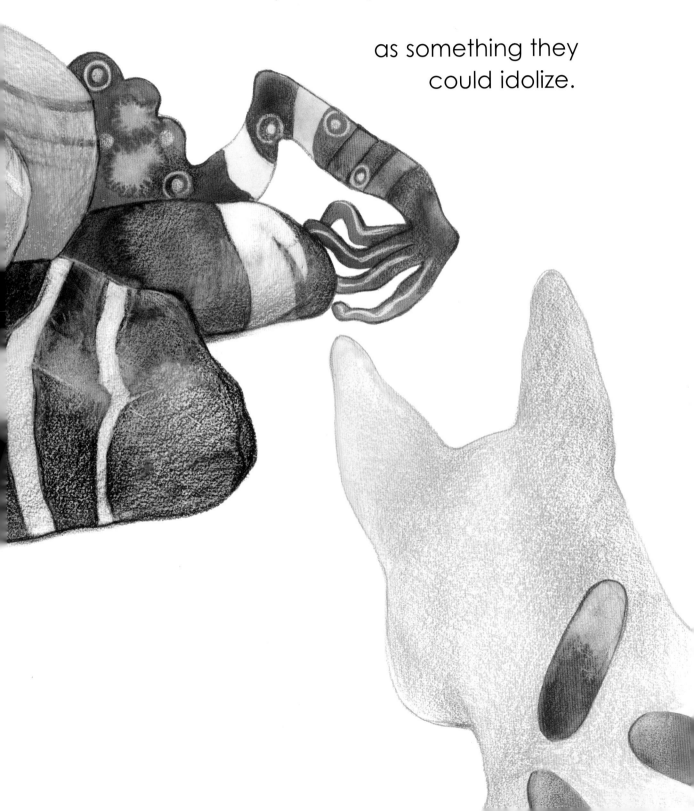

The fourth smallest lemmie
was sorely perplexed;

if he tested this thing,
what might it do next?

Just slithering out
was enough of a shock;

it was better
sequestered
behind the rock.

The fifth smallest lemmie
            decided to greet

the troublesome toad
            and say something sweet.

The largest of the lemmies

then led the rest,

confronting with courage a
conceivable pest.

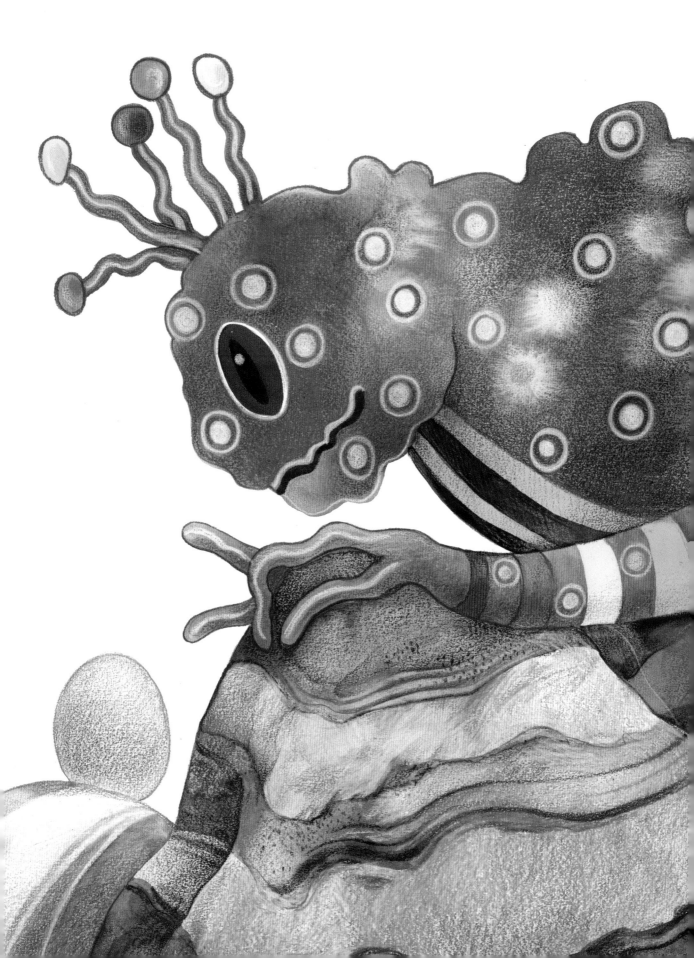

And heard it attest in a voice
deep and mean,

"You're the worst looking creeps
I have ever seen!"

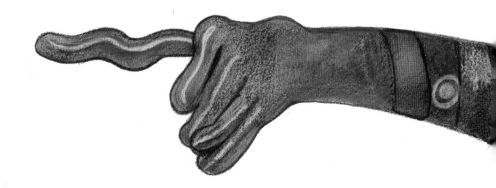

The lemmies, now tearful, rejected,

departed despondent, dejected,

in shambles groped homeward,

immoderately shaken,

and hoped that the toad was
a little mistaken.

This book contributes to the hope that people will one day treat one another with the patience, tolerance and understanding required to realize a more comfortable and happier world. No child is too young, no adult too old, to join in this optimistic endeavor.

AK & KK

Arnold Klein majored in English literature and art history at Hamilton College, Clinton, New York and earned an M.A. in French from Columbia University. He taught at St. Paul's School in Concord, New Hampshire and the University of Detroit, and was curatorial assistant at the Detroit Institute of Arts. Presently, he is co-owner and director of Arnold Klein Gallery, Royal Oak, Michigan.

Karen Klein's B.S. in design is from the University of Michigan and her M.A. from Wayne State University. She works primarily in watercolor and color pencil, makes artist's books and has exhibited in Michigan, Ohio, New York and Washington, D.C. Her works are in the Minneapolis Institute of Arts, the New York Public Library and the Detroit Institute of Arts. She is co-owner of Arnold Klein Gallery.